# The Nightingale

# HANS CHRISTIAN ANDERSEN

# The Nightingale

## ILLUSTRATED BY

## Demi

A VOYAGER / HBJ BOOK

HARCOURT BRACE JOVANOVICH, PUBLISHERS

SAN DIEGO   NEW YORK   LONDON

Thanks are due to Tze-Si "Jesse" Huang
for the Chinese calligraphy
and to Simon Ho for mounting
on rice paper the Chinese silk
containing the color art.

LIBRARY OF CONGRESS CATALOGING IN PUBLICATION DATA
Andersen, H. C. (Hans Christian), 1805–1875. The nightingale.

Translation of: Nattergalen.
SUMMARY: Though the emperor banishes the nightingale in
preference for a jeweled mechanical imitation, the little
bird remains faithful and returns years later when the
emperor is near death and no one else can help him.
1. Children's stories, Danish. [1. Fairy tales.
2. Nightingales—Fiction] I. Demi, ill. II. Title.
PZ8.A542Ni 1985 [E] 85–2765
ISBN 0-15-257427-1
ISBN 0-15-257428-X (pbk.)
PRINTED AND BOUND BY SOUTH CHINA PRINTING COMPANY, QUARRY BAY, HONG KONG
A B C D E

碧安娜

FOR ANNA BIER

HE PALACE of the Emperor of China was the most splendid in the world. It was made of priceless porcelain that was both brittle and delicate. Anyone who touched it, therefore, had to be very careful.

The garden was filled with beautiful flowers, and on the loveliest of them were tied silver bells. Their tinkling made a wonderful sound, and anyone who passed by could not help admiring the flowers.

Everything was arranged to please the eye, and the garden was so large that even the gardener did not know where it ended.

Beyond it, however, lay a stately forest with great trees and deep lakes. The forest sloped down to the sea, which was a clear blue. Large ships could sail under the branches of the trees, and in the trees lived a nightingale. She sang so beautifully that even a poor fisherman, who had too much to do, stood and listened when he came at night to cast his nets. "How beautiful!" he said, but then he had to go back to his work. He forgot about the bird, but when he came back the next night and heard her sing, he said again, "How beautiful!"

Travelers from many countries came to admire the palace and the garden, but when they heard the nightingale sing, they all said, "This is the finest thing in all the kingdom."

When they returned home, they told about all they had seen, and scholars wrote books about the city, the palace, and garden, praising the nightingale above everything else. Poets also composed splendid verses about the nightingale in the forest by the sea.

Eventually some of the books reached the Emperor. He sat on his golden chair and read and read. He nodded his head from time to time, for he enjoyed reading about the city, the palace, and the garden. But when he came to the words, "But the nightingale is best of all," he was amazed.

"What is that?" said the Emperor. "I don't know anything about such a bird in my kingdom. I have never heard it! Fancy learning about it for the first time in a book!"

He called his First Lord. "There is a most remarkable bird called a nightingale in the forest," he said. "The book says it is the most glorious thing in my kingdom. Why has no one ever said anything to me about it?"

"I have never heard it mentioned," said the First Lord. "I will look for it and find it."

But where was it to be found? The First Lord ran upstairs and downstairs, through the halls and corridors, but no one he met had ever heard of the nightingale. He eventually went back to the Emperor and told him it must be an invention on the part of those who had written the books.

"But the book in which I read this," said the Emperor, "was sent to me by the Emperor of Japan. It cannot be untrue, and I will hear this nightingale. She has my gracious permission to appear this evening, and if she does not, the whole court shall be beaten."

The First Lord and half the court searched and searched. At last they met a poor kitchen maid who said, "Oh, I know the nightingale. I am allowed to carry food left over from the court meals to my sick mother. When I go home at night, tired and weary, and stop to rest in the woods, I hear the nightingale singing. She brings tears to my eyes, and I feel as if my mother were kissing me."

"Little kitchen maid," said the First Lord. "I will give you a good place in the kitchen and permission to see the Emperor at dinner if you can lead us to the nightingale. She is invited to the court this evening."

And so they set out for the forest, and half the court went too.

On the way they heard a cow mooing.

"Oh," said one of the courtiers, "we have found her. What a wonderful voice for such a small creature!"

"No, that is a cow mooing," said the kitchen maid. "We still have a long way to go."

Then the frogs began to croak in the marsh. "Splendid," said the chaplain. "Her voice sounds like church bells."

"No, no, those are frogs," said the kitchen maid. "But I think we shall soon hear her."

Then the nightingale began to sing. "There she is!" cried the little kitchen maid. "Listen! She is sitting there." And she pointed to a little gray bird up in the branches.

"Is it possible?" said the First Lord. "How ordinary she looks! Seeing so many distinguished people around must have made her lose her color."

"Little nightingale," called the kitchen maid. "Our Gracious Emperor wants you to sing for him."

"With the greatest pleasure!" said the nightingale, and she sang so gloriously that it was a pleasure to listen.

"It sounds like glass bells!" said the First Lord. "And look how her little throat works. She will be a great success at court."

"Shall I sing once more for the Emperor?" asked the nightingale, thinking that the Emperor was there.

"My esteemed little nightingale," said the First Lord. "I have the great pleasure of inviting you to the court this evening, where His Gracious Imperial Highness will be enchanted with your song."

"It sounds best in the green woods," said the nightingale, but she came willingly when she heard the Emperor wished it.

At the palace everything was in readiness. The porcelain walls and floors glittered in the light of thousands of gold lamps, and there was such a hustle and bustle that the silver bells placed on the flowers in the corridors jingled constantly.

In the center of the great hall where the Emperor sat, a golden perch had been set up for the nightingale. The whole court was in attendance, including the little kitchen maid, who had been promoted to a cook. Everyone was looking at the little gray bird.

When the Emperor nodded, the nightingale began her song. She sang so gloriously that tears came into the Emperor's eyes and ran down his cheeks. Then she sang even more beautifully, touching the hearts of all who heard her. The Emperor was so delighted that he suggested she wear his golden slipper around her neck.

The nightingale thanked him but said she had had enough reward already. "I have seen tears in the Emperor's eyes."

She was a great success. All the court ladies tried to imitate the nightingale by holding water in their mouths to make a gurgling sound whenever someone spoke to them. Eleven grocers' children were named after her, even though not one of them could sing a note.

Now the nightingale had to stay at court. She had her own cage and was allowed to take a walk twice a day and once at night. She could not enjoy flying, however, because the twelve servants she had been given each held a silken string fastened around her leg.

One day the Emperor received a large parcel on which was written: *The Nightingale*.

"Here is another book about our famous bird," said the Emperor. It was not a book, however, but a mechanical toy lying in a box—an artificial nightingale that looked like the real one but was covered with diamonds, rubies, and sapphires. When the artificial bird was wound up, it could sing as sweetly as the real nightingale and could move its glittering silver and gold tail up and down, as well.

Round its neck was a little collar on which was written: *The nightingale of the Emperor of Japan is nothing compared to that of the Emperor of China.*

"Now they must sing together," ordered the Emperor. "What a duet we shall have!"

Their voices did not blend, however. The real nightingale sang in her own way, and the artificial bird sang only waltzes.

"The new bird is not at fault," said the music master. "It keeps very good time and does its job well."

Then the artificial bird sang alone. It gave as much pleasure as the real nightingale and was much prettier to look at with its sparkling jewels. Three and thirty times it sang the same piece without tiring. People would have liked to hear it again, but the Emperor thought it was time for the real nightingale to sing again. But she was nowhere to be found. No one had noticed that she had flown out the open window.

"What shall we do?" asked the Emperor.

The members of the court called the real nightingale ungrateful and said, "But we still have the best songbird!"

Then for the thirty-fourth time they heard the same piece, but they still did not know it because it was much too difficult. The music master assured them that the artificial bird was better than the real nightingale. "My lords and ladies and your Imperial Majesty, with the real nightingale one can never tell what song will come out, but everything is in perfect order with the artificial bird. You can examine its mechanism and see how it operates."

"That is just what we think," said all the courtiers.

The music master was then given permission to show the bird to the people the next Sunday. When they heard it, they were enchanted and nodded time with their forefingers. But the poor fisherman who had heard the real nightingale said, "This one sings well enough. The tunes glide out, but there is something wanting—I don't know what."

The real nightingale was banished from the kingdom.

The artificial bird was put on silken cushions near the Emperor's bed, and all the presents it received, gold and precious stones, lay around it. It was given the title of Imperial Night Singer.

The music master wrote twenty-five volumes about the artificial bird. They were so learned and long that all the people pretended they had read and understood them, for they did not want to appear stupid and be flogged for it as had happened in the past.

A whole year passed. The Emperor, the court, and the people knew every note of the artificial bird's songs. They preferred it that way because they could sing along with the bird.

But one evening, while the artificial bird was singing for the Emperor, something snapped. The music ceased. The Emperor sprang up and summoned his physician, but what could *he* do? Then the clockmaker came, and he managed to put the bird somewhat back in order. He said, however, that it must be used very seldom since the works were nearly worn out and it was impossible to put in new ones.

Only once a year was the artificial bird allowed to sing, and even that one performance was almost too much for it. Five years passed, and then a great sorrow befell the country. The Emperor became ill, and it was reported that he was unlikely to recover. Already a new Emperor had been chosen.

Cold and pale, the Emperor lay on his bed. The whole court believed him dead, and everyone went to pay respects to the new Emperor. Cloth was laid down in the corridors so that no footstep could be heard, and everything was very still.

The Emperor longed for something to relieve the monotony of the deathlike silence. If only someone would speak to him or sing to him! Music would break the spell that enveloped him. Moonlight was streaming in the open window, but that, too, was quite silent.

"Music! Music!" cried the Emperor. "You bright golden bird, sing! I gave you gold and jewels and hung my gold slipper around your neck. Sing, do sing!" But the bird was silent. There was no one to wind it up, and so it could not sing. All was silent, so terribly silent!

All at once there came through the window the most glorious burst of song. It was the real nightingale, who was sitting in the tree outside his window. She had heard of the Emperor's illness and had come to sing to him of comfort and hope. As she sang, the blood flowed more and more quickly through the Emperor's body and life began to return.

"Thank you, thank you!" said the Emperor. "You divine little bird! I know you. I chased you from my kingdom, and you have given me life again. How can I reward you?"

"You have done that already," said the nightingale. "I brought tears to your eyes the first time I sang. I shall never forget that. They are the jewels that gladden a singer's heart. But now sleep and get strong again; I will sing you a lullaby." And the Emperor fell into a deep, calm sleep as she sang.

The sun was shining through the window when he awoke, strong and well. None of his servants had come back yet, for they thought he was dead. But the nightingale sat and sang to him.

"You must stay with me always," said the Emperor. "You shall sing whenever you like, and I will break the artificial bird into a thousand pieces."

"Don't do that!" said the nightingale. "He did his work as long as he could. Keep him. I cannot build my nest in the palace and live here, but let me come whenever I like. In the evening I will sit outside your window and sing you something that will make you feel happy and grateful.

"I will sing of joy and of sorrow, of the evil and the good that lies hidden from you. A singing bird flies all over, to the poor fisherman's hut, to the farmer's cottage, to all those who are far away from you and your court. I love your heart more than your crown, though that has about it a brightness as of something holy. Now I will sing to you again, but you must promise me one thing—"

"Anything!" said the Emperor, standing up in his imperial robes, which he himself had put on, and fastening on his sword richly embossed with gold.

"One thing I beg of you. Don't tell anyone that you have a little bird who tells you everything. It will be much better not to." Then the nightingale flew away.

Later that morning everyone was astonished to see the Emperor step out on his balcony and with his great deep voice firmly greet one and all with a grand "Good morning!"

The text for *The Nightingale* was adapted by Anna Bier from
the 1894 edition of *The Yellow Fairy Book* edited by Andrew Lang
and published by Longmans, Green, and Company. The adaptation
remains quite faithful to the original, but some passages have been
deleted and others altered to make the text read
more smoothly and to remove obscurities.

The base line art was prepared first. Then
the color paintings were prepared on fine, brilliant
Wu silk, which is closely and wonderfully woven.
Traditional Chinese paints were used. The blues and greens
came from azurite, malachite, and indigo; the reds from cinnabar,
realgar, and orpiment, with the brilliant red from coral and the pink-
red from a flowering vine; umber from an iron oxide called limonite;
yellow from the sap of the rattan plant; and white from lead or
pulverized oyster shells. To all, powdered jade was added for good
fortune. These colors were mixed with stag horn, fish or ox glue,
or glue made from the pulp of the soap bean. The black Chinese ink
is ten parts pine soot, three parts powdered jade, and one part glue
made from donkey hides boiled in Tung River water.

The paints were mixed with boiling water. In the first stage
the water looked like fish eyes; in the second, like innumerable
pearls strung together; and in the final stage, like rolling breakers.
The paints were then applied with Chinese brushes made of sheep,
rabbit, goat, weasel, and wolf hairs picked in autumn, as well as of
mouse whiskers, with handles of bamboo and buffalo horn.
Where changes were required in the art, the paint was removed
by wiping the area with the juice of the apricot seed.

The Linotype Caslon and Delphin No. 1 display were composed by
Maryland Linotype Composition Company, Baltimore, Maryland.
Color separations were made by
Heinz Weber, Inc., Los Angeles, California.

PRINTED IN HONG KONG

A VOYAGER/HBJ BOOK

HARCOURT BRACE JOVANOVICH, PUBLISHERS

1250 SIXTH AVENUE, SAN DIEGO, CA 92101

111 FIFTH AVENUE, NEW YORK, NY 10003

ISBN 0-15-257428-X